MUSINGS

SANGEETHA PUZHAKKAL

To amma and achan

Contents

musings

Sangeetha Puzhakkal

Cover and Illustrations

by Sangeetha Puzhakkal

About The Author

Sangeetha Puzhakkal

From north Kerala, studied in Malappuram, Ranchi, Delhi and Kochi. Loves the world of words and colours. Faculty at TKM College, Kollam, Kerala. Lives with family in Kollam.

Acknowledgements

A few lines penned down at intervals with the prodding of loved ones have become this little book. I would like to thank my entire family and friends for their kind words of encouragement especially my parents, Shantha and Appukuttan, mother-in-law, Mochi aunty (Usha Narendran), brothers Sanjay and Sanjeev, husband Ramesh and son Arjun who first instilled some confidence in me to begin writing.

On this occasion I remember with gratitude, late Prof. Abdul Ali, Feroke, who suggested that I get the stories published. I also want to thank my friends Amulya, Rajeswari, Shivani and Bibi for helping me in this venture.

Deeply indebted to Joji, editor and publisher of Nishagandhi Publications, Irinjalakuda, who took the initiative and gave the courage to go ahead with this venture and who first published the book. Thank you Anakha and Priyanka of Notion Press Publishers and your team for your great support in getting the book through to the second edition. Thank you everyone.

KAMALEDATHI AMONG OTHERS

As my thoughts take an occasional dip in the pond of childhood memories, the ripples bring to mind many pictures - one of those is of Kamaledathi.

So clearly can I picture her walking towards our house from far away, from where I could also see the giant mango tree which stood majestically and provided us with so many beautiful memories of hours spent under its shelter playing all sorts of games, reading, listening to stories told by older cousins, squabbling or nibbling at mangoes. The babble of children's voices continue to ring in my ears as my mind relives those days when we took turns on the swing that hung from a high sturdy branch, the height inhibiting the little ones from clambering onto it.

My childish mind foolishly believed that the gentle, cool breeze that stole upon us, surprising us with its suddenness and bringing a welcome short relief on those sultry sweaty afternoons began its journey from near the mango tree.

Those were the little 'big' joys of childhood when we chanced upon a smooth odd-shaped pebble, a curiously shaped insect or differently patterned leaves. Raindrops falling rhythmically in the courtyard during those seemingly endless monsoons, playing with droplets of water on large chembu* leaves, the harvest season, and the ensuing excitement. The mind begins to wander again. A face sets off a stream of memories.

Tall, upright Kamaledathi, her fair face glistening with sweat, carrying a huge pile of firewood, this balancing act would make us look at her with amazement each time she passed us. However, she would always smile nodding her head at us, her brows knit together and forehead creased with the burden on her head.

Afternoons would find her on the kitchen veranda with rice piled high on her plate. This mountain of rice (it seemed so then) earned her the nickname 'petu'*. Although the elders admonished us for calling her by that name then, the name stuck. Whenever her name came up in our conversation, 'petu' would precede it. Strangely the only other work that I remember her doing was filling up the innumerable vessels lined up near the well though I am sure she assisted in several other chores around the house.

Strongly built, she was said to be a good worker as she never dawdled but would go about her work briskly and only stop for a minute or two to drink water. I remember someone saying how to everyone's surprise she didn't turn up for work one day and on enquiry, it was found that she had had a baby. It turned out that the previous day although asked to leave early she had stayed back to pound rice.

Chanduchan who used to cut grandfather's hair was someone who knew exactly when he was expected. A timid man, he seemed to become more nervous in the imposing presence of grandpa. He would take out his tools from a wooden box with a sliding lid that he carried and would also feed grandpa the local news as he set about his work.

His low voice almost like a murmur was not audible to us children but would be punctuated by the loud grunts of grandpa. Once we all had a taste of Chanduchan's 'haircut'. Summer had begun and the elders decided that the children needed to shorten their hair. After Chanduchan left, except the older cousins all of us were teary eyed as all our bald heads were gleaming in the afternoon light. After that, I remember we would step out with great caution when Chanduchan arrived.

There stood a croton tree in the courtyard. It was a fairly large tree with multi-hued leaves. My little brother would be often taken there by my grandpa when he was crying or in an irritable mood. The myriad colours of the tree distracted my brother and grandpa would point to the leaves and ask, "do you want this light green one? Or that yellow one?" It was fascinating to watch the transformation of the duo, one who only a minute ago had been bawling and the other, my grandpa, who inspired awe in people showing so much tenderness, which was rare. Although stern with his own children he was a very doting grandfather. Occasions like these brought out the wealth of love that lay hidden in him which were well masked albeit unconsciously. His booming voice, the creases on his large forehead, his sharp nose and gaze added to his grim expression. But there were times when he broke out into loud laughter and his face would assume a childlike expression.

Not very far from the croton tree stood the well which was forbidden territory for the smaller children. Finding everyone enjoying their siesta, one day my elder brother slipped stealthily from his bed and reached the well. Very quietly he started drawing water. Suddenly on spotting a chameleon on the wall of the well, he let go of the rope and bolted. The rope made a screeching sound as it rubbed against the pulley. The bucket of water landed in the deep well with a lot of noise. Hearing the sound of the bucket hitting the water the household woke up. With the child missing and the bucket in the water, my mother almost swooned. My brother, watching the chaos from behind a tree realized that the situation was getting out of hand and softly called out, "amma" It took some time to coax him from the hiding place, "The chameleon stared at me," he sheepishly admitted later.
Andiyettan who looked after the cattle always had a gentle smile playing on his lips. I remember how in the mornings my younger brother would tumble out of bed and head straight for the shed where the oxen were. He would play with their horns and pat their faces and hug them sitting comfortably on the itchy yellow hay which would stick out from his ears, hair and neck as they, in turn, licked his little face and hands with their rough purplish tongues. It was such a cozy, joyful scene and although tempted to follow him I would only watch from

a safe distance. The reassuring presence of Andiyettan was enough to ward off any apprehensions amma might have had about his safety.

Soon we moved to the city, our visits only an annual affair, dwindling to occasional and saw little of Kamaledathi and other old familiar faces like that of Kuttayettan, the boatman who would help us to get in and out of the boat, ever silent and patient. How many he had ferried across the river, men, women and children. He knew each one of them and listened to the conversations saying little, seemingly immersed in his thoughts.

All of them have moved on as has Kamaledathi and become things of the past. The mango tree stands there no more and many of the voices have also faded into oblivion. Those who were once part and parcel of our lives now live in the cobweb of our memories brought out only sparingly as we trudge the familiar and sometimes not so familiar path laid before us with little time to spare for such trivialities and so they lie there, forgotten, gathering dust, as have those before them and those to follow.

CHAPTER TWO

ALI

Ali was thinking hard. Abdul could see that. On such occasions, he would walk straight and quick like an arrow.

He found it difficult to keep pace with him.

What had got into him? Something had disturbed his younger brother. The last time this happened was when he had an argument with his teacher. If he believed he was right there was no stopping him. The fact that they had not taken the regular path made walking all the more difficult. The brambles clung to his clothes.

There were sharp pebbles and thorns which hurt his slipper-less feet. Ali seemed oblivious to it all.

Abdul could never fathom this queer behavior of Ali.

Though younger to him by nearly two years Ali was the boss.

Abdul disliked friction of any sort and would give in to his brother's little whims and fancies. But at the same time, his father seemed to take pride in him. "He is a little lion cub, so much like my bapa* and my ikka.* He has fire in him," he would tell his wife.

Abdul's uncle Abdullah took care of the family property and all the work related to it. His father never involved himself with anything if he could help it. The few times he had seen his father intervene was when he wanted to address the woes of someone who worked for them. Thus, the brothers were a picture of contrast. His gentle, peace-loving father Hameed looked after the affairs of the school. The rest of the time he would be among his books and papers.

Soon they reached the clearing which was the backyard of their house. This was the easiest way to reach the house from school. While Abdul went to wash himself near the well, Ali flung his books onto the old wooden bench. The rubber band that had held the books together broke. "Umma," called out Ali. "Wash and come, tea is ready," answered his mother from the kitchen. "Where is bapa? I want to see him first," he said. "Must be in the front veranda." she replied from inside.

Ali stomped to the front of the house followed by Abdul who knew the puzzle would unravel now. "bapa...how can you...how can you...?" He was too overcome by emotion to speak further.

His face had turned red. Tears were running down his cheeks.

bapa had been dozing on the reclining chair. He knew his son was upset. He stretched out his hands to pat his eight-year-old son but Ali brushed it aside angrily. He told Abdul to fetch a glass of water for him. "Sit," he said indicating a stool near him. At first Ali hesitated, then sat down. His father handed him a towel to wipe his face. "Now tell me," he said gently.

Ali was quiet for a few seconds. After handing over the glass of water to Ali, Abdul stood by leaning against the wall. His umma had not heard the commotion. "Why is food served in the pit for the workers? Why can't they eat like us? Food is thrown at them...as though...as though...they are dogs." He finished hoarsely.

Abdul stood perplexed. The fact that they had made a detour may annoy his father. This was the second time that they had decided to be adventurous. Although he had come here where the workers were having lunch before, he had never felt anything amiss.

Today, the discussion in school had been about the goat and kid that Rahim's father had bought. Ali had insisted on seeing them. Abdul had been a little wary of taking this way. The last time he had been chased by a hen or was it a cockerel? He had not seen it well. It was all over in seconds. It had scratched and pecked him all over. He had fallen down in a heap. It was Ali who had come to his rescue. He had caught hold of it and yanked it away. The lady of the house had come running, helped him get up, washed and cleaned his wounds, and taken them home. What was she explaining to umma about the hen being kept for sacrifice and that there had been some delay and it had turned violent? He couldn't make head or tail of what had been said. He was bruised all over and it was stinging. His mother had made him a hot concoction and put him to bed.

So, after they had spent some time with the goat and kids, they had decided to take the same route. For this, they had to cross the paddy field that belonged to them. The first time Abdul accompanied his father there, he had been fascinated by the sight of plantain leaves thrown on the pits upon which food was served. All the men sat near their pit to eat. Afterwards the remains were pushed into the pit and covered. What a novel idea! And they had eaten so fast! Perhaps they had been very hungry. His umma would always chide them if they gulped down food. This they did whenever summoned to eat in the middle of a game.

As they stood watching Abdul could see that Ali's expression had changed. It was the first time that Ali had come here and he looked agitated. What could be wrong? Suddenly Ali had turned away and started walking.

Abdul could see now that his father looked thoughtful. But that was an almost permanent expression on his father's face especially when he was composing poems of which they understood very little.

Hameed's mind was reliving a similar scene that had taken place so many years ago. He had been probably around the same age as his young son who sat before him looking at him expectantly with red-rimmed eyes. He remembered that he had asked the same question to his father who had glared at him so hard that he had hidden behind his mother. His father had been an overpowering personality like his brother.

Many years later this was one of the suggestions he had made to his brother of whom he was not so afraid. His brother had dismissed it. There had been no further discussions so he had given in and gone back to his books and poetry.

But Ali was different. He would fight it. All he needed was a backing. And he will provide it, thought Hameed, "Come son, let's go out. We need to buy some things," he said heading into his room to change.

The following day all the workers were eating in plates. Abdullah was furious. Whose idea is this? He thundered. "Ali's," said Hameed quietly looking into his eyes. Abdullah stood like one turned to stone, not a word did he utter.

CHAPTER THREE

GRANDMA'S TALE

As Veena watched the clothes drying in the clothesline something tugged at her heart, a mixture of sadness and contentment. Her mind flew to that Friday afternoon. Nandini and she had been walking to the Science block to meet her sister. It was raining quite heavily.

This fifteen-minute walk from the Arts block was made often as many of their classmate's siblings studied there. They were sharing an umbrella between them as Veena had forgotten to bring her umbrella. Veena was very forgetful so this happened frequently and they usually ended up getting wet. Today was no exception. Avoiding the puddles as they walked along with the rain lashing around them, she was straining to hear what Nandini was saying. For one, she spoke really fast. She was a good narrator and loved to talk. The rain drumming down on the umbrella did not help at all.

Nandini had lived with her grandma in Madras ever since she had been little. On one of her visits, she had had a fall and the doctor had advised complete rest and to her grandma's delight it was decided that she should stay on. Her mother required some persuasion to let her stay on in Madras and had finally only half-heartedly agreed. A world of good it had done for both as her grandma was alone and Nandini was a cheerful, mischievous and exuberant child that grandma found difficult to contain at times. Her two younger siblings lived with her parents here where now she had come to do her graduation.

She missed her grandma terribly. Almost everything would remind her of her grandma and her name often popped up in their conversations.

"My grandma's sister had got married," began Nandini. It had been less than a year in a far-off village in North Kerala. Grandma lived in Madras then. She gets a telegram one day saying her sister was critical," Nandini's voice was drowned in loud honking. An auto guy glared. Totally engrossed in their conversation they had stepped on to the road. "Sorry," said Veena and they edged sideways.

"Okay and then?" she turned to Nandini. "Oh nothing, by the time she reached everything was over. Someone said the fire had been an accident. The only other relative who had accompanied my grandma was an elderly cousin. Although they suspected foul play, they felt it was pointless pursuing it as her sister was gone. There were some rituals for grandma's sister that they had to attend so they stayed on. But a strange thing happened."

Veena peered to read Nandini's expression. Her glasses were wet, she could barely see her face. By then they had reached the gates of the college where Nandini's sister met them. After giving her the book, they started back to the Arts block.

"Alright and then?" asked Veena. "Guess what! I was supposed to meet Sr. Frances at the library," said Nandini slapping her forehead. So they folded their umbrellas and broke into a run. The heavy downpour had anyway turned to a drizzle.

Veena sat through the rest of the lectures impatiently. Classes over, another friend joined them in their walk to the bus stop. So Veena had to wait till the next day to hear the rest of the story.

When they met for lunch the following day, Nandini continued from where she had stopped. "As I said, my grandma stayed on for a few days till the rituals were complete. One day after her bath she was putting out clothes on the line and suddenly finds this apparition on the other side.

Her hair in disarray, her face and clothes blackened with soot and with such a sad expression on her face, grandma said she would never forget till her last breath. And then it disappeared."

"Wouldn't she have imagined it? You know, obviously she must have been in a shock and all," Veena had asked after a few moments. "The same thought had occurred to me also but grandma said she had not been thinking of her sister at all when this happened. There had been a knot at the end of her saree which she had overlooked while washing. She had been intent on untying it." "Oh" said Veena and then fell silent. They were startled when suddenly the bell rang and they went to their respective classes.

Years later when she got a call from her cousin, was it this tale that had prompted Veena to rush to her, give her support and courage to get a legal separation from her husband and start life anew? Although her aunt and uncle had vehemently opposed it and her own parents were wavering they had managed it. Today her cousin was leading life on her own terms and reasonably happy.

"Time I caught up with Nandini," she mused as she picked up the clothes and folded them away neatly. They had not met since college. There was so much to catch up on, she thought as she glanced up casually across the clothes line. No, that was the shadow of the creeper growing overhead. There was no one standing on the other side. Veena smiled to herself.

CHAPTER FOUR

GIRI MAMA

We often met Giri mama either in the lift or would bump into him in the long corridors of the building where we met most of the hundred odd residents of our building. He had a pleasant, bright thoughtful face that lit up and broke into a smile whenever he met an acquaintance and only an acquaintance I had been then till the incident that happened during Holi.

The kids of the building are in a boisterous mood come Holi. For them the celebrations begin weeks before. Balloons filled with coloured water are thrown at all and sundry. Little gangs would suddenly appear from nowhere amidst riotous laughter and charge like a bunch of red Indians to find a victim. One day the prank went too far. It so happened that one of their unsuspecting victims happened to be Giri mama who was on his way to his flat located on the third floor of the building.

His bright sunlit face and his shiny bald pate glinting in the sun must have attracted one of the boys who threw a bottle at him. It had been an impulsive act but the deed was done and the children became afraid and made themselves scarce. The last of them however decided to take another look and was spotted by a neighbor who had come to assist the bleeding Giri mama. The boys happened to have been standing in the corridor right outside our flat so hither he came to complain. Enquiries were made. It was the bunch of which my brother was party to.

The entire lot of them from four-year-olds to fourteen-year-olds were marched to Giri Mama and asked to tender an apology. As they stood before him shamefaced, he only smiled and said that anyone would have been tempted to do it given the hairless state of his head. Fortunately, he wasn't too hurt. The bottle had grazed his head and smashed to the ground.

Giri mama's warm, gentle demeanor won everyone's heart. He was popular among the children and other residents in the building. Everyone would stop to chat with him even if for a minute or two. His endearing smile won the hearts of toddlers and the elderly alike. Thus it was that when he suffered a heart attack everyone in the building was concerned. We had known that he was a heart patient but this was a major attack. His son Harish flew in from Chhindwara where his family lived.

Giri mama's wife Prema couldn't come as there were elderly parents at home. Egged on by the ministrations of his doting son, Giri mama was soon on the road to recovery.

One day, I visited him along with my brother in the hospital but hid the rose I had brought for him when I saw the beautiful bouquets arranged near his bedside. Giri mama, being an important person in the government, had many official visitors. My brother however let the cat out of the bag and I was forced to produce the rose which had by then half-withered in my tightly clad fist. He smilingly reached for it and pinned it on his shirt front. "This is so much more precious than all the flowers put together," he said. My eyes filled up at this juncture and I had a hard time trying to keep my composure. Only the previous week had I chided myself for my embarrassing public performances as the waterworks refuse to stop once it started but it had not done any good.

Once he was back in his flat, I was a regular visitor, sometimes reading the newspaper for him, at times quietly listening to him talk. I remember once going to him after a game of cricket. The ball had hit my wrist and a red bangle I was wearing had cracked. I was a little upset as I had bought it during the annual festival at our family temple during our previous vacation and looking at it brought back memories of the wonderful time we had during our summer vacation at my father's village in Kerala. As we spoke he must have absently put it into his coat pocket for there he found it the following year and returned it to me.

Time went by, Giri mama retired and went back to Chhindwara. Many of us left the building, though with promises of keeping in touch, rarely did we hear from anyone. It so happened that a close relative was getting married in Nagpur. As it was not very far from Chhindwaara we decided to meet up with Giri mama and family. We had kept in touch with him through occasional phone calls and letters and were excited about seeing him in person. He was also looking forward to meeting us.

We were greeted by him and Prema aunty at the door. We looked around eagerly for Harish and his family. He had always spoken about them and he used to get very vocal when it came to his grandson. But they were nowhere to be seen. Following our gaze, Giri mama told us that since they had a function to attend, Harish and family couldn't make it. We had assumed that they lived together. Giri mama explained that they had until Pranav started going to school when they moved to a flat closer to his school. We spent a few hours with them reminiscing about old common acquaintances. Most of their conversation centered around Pranav but a veil of sadness clung to their words. It was clear that they missed him dearly. They had also wanted us to meet him. "What is to be done?" said aunty, "Young folks these days like to stay by themselves, old houses, old people are a nuisance." she said half to herself with a sigh. "Pranav's school bus goes this way... if they wanted," she continued. Giri mama interrupted unexpectedly, "Harish's office is also very close to their flat." He then changed the topic.

It was then that I noticed that the old twinkle was gone from his eyes. The once sunny face was overshadowed by worry lines. He had aged considerably. But it had been only ten years, I wondered. Soon it was time to leave. We promised to visit again and said goodbye. Both of them stood near the gate, two lonely figures in their twilight years, to see us off.

We sat in the train on our way back to Nagpur, each of us absorbed in our thoughts. Somehow our hearts felt heavy. Our attention was diverted by the sound of gurgling baby laughter. Everyone watched the mother and child, totally absorbed in themselves. The mother would say something which would set the child off into peals of laughter. The father sat by watching and smiled encouragingly. A pretty picture.

As the train picked up speed, I averted my gaze from the duo and dug my hand into my handbag to take out a book to read. And that was when my hand closed upon the little red glass bangle which I remembered to take at the last moment to show Giri mama. It had completely slipped my mind. The once shiny bangle had lost all its lustre and sheen and lay desolate in my palm, the crack now standing out more clearly than ever.

CHAPTER FIVE

AMJAD'S WORLD

Little Amjad sat cross-legged on the string cot in the inner courtyard of his house. The pale moon cast shadows around him. All was quiet in the village except for the occasional bleat of a goat or the bark of a dog. The villagers slept early. It was well past Amjad's bedtime. But today sleep was eluding him. It had been an exciting as well as a disturbing day. His mind had been in a whirl.

It had all begun with Hassan *chacha's visit. The heat was a bit stifling this afternoon and he had dozed off. He woke up to hear someone talking. Hassan chacha was talking in a low voice to ammi and his grandparents. His mother sat expressionlessly. His grandparents seemed to stare blankly at Hassan chacha's face. It was unlikely that they followed what was being said. They barely understood what was happening at home. Hassan chacha stopped talking as soon as Amjad entered. Hassan chacha had been his abba's best friend who had dreamed the American dream, done very well for himself and settled there.

Since his father's death when Amjad was six, Hassan chacha would only pay short visits whenever he came on his annual visit to India. On earlier visits most of his time was spent with his friend. They had studied together in school as well as in college and were also neighbours. Whenever he visited, he would bring toys or clothes for Amjad and something for his grandparents. Amjad often wondered about the place that produced such fine things and which earned him the envious looks of his friends and classmates.

Soon after Hassan chacha left, his ammi* told him that he had come with a proposal. He wanted to help them in some way, now that their only breadwinner abba* was gone. Since he had no children of his own, he wished to adopt Amjad, educate him and help him to have a successful career and life. This was the least he could do for a dear friend who had been his soul mate. Amjad was a bright-eyed, intelligent and level headed boy. Anyone could see, that given the right guidance and push he would do well in life. His mother however wanted the decision to be purely his. She did not want to influence him in any way and be a hindrance to his prospects.

Amjad could not read his mother's mind. Her tone betrayed no emotion. But that was the way her mother had always been especially after abba died. She never raised her voice. The calm composure of his ammi gave him a feeling of security. Ammi saw to all his needs but sometimes he wished that abba was around somewhere. He had been full of life and would throw him up in the air and catch him. He could still see his mother watching openmouthed. That was something she didn't approve of. It frightened her. But he did it anyway and Amjad enjoyed it too. It was quite exhilarating. The only other time he had felt the same was when he took a ride in the giant wheel. The same feeling had swept over him. He had suddenly missed his father then.

It was Hassan chacha who had taken him to the local fair. Chachi also seemed nice, with kind eyes and a ready smile. They had bought him a lot of things and had taken all the rides a seven-year-old could take. In many ways, Hassan chacha reminded him of his abba especially when he would take him in his lap. Hassan chacha had often described to him among other things about the amusement parks where they lived and it seemed like a magical place to Amjad.

This was Amjad's favourite spot. This was where he would retreat when he wanted to be left alone. His mother always encouraged him to play outside with his friends. She did not like to see him brood. Conversations were few and far between them in the house. His mother worked from early morning till sundown.

Then they read the namaz together and spoke a little among themselves. Although their house was small it was cool and comfortable and gave protection from the blazing sun outside. His grandfather had withdrawn into a shell and only answered in monosyllables to their queries. His grandma would ask about his school, his friends, and whether he had taken his meals. That was all. They would sit together watching the embers in the firewood burn itself out and then go to sleep.

Now sitting here after his dinner of daal and rotis he pondered over what his mother had told him. He liked Hassan chacha. He was like a father figure to him. America which had seemed a distant dream was now only a stone's throw away. This was probably the chance of a lifetime. Wouldn't it be wonderful to live in a large house with a beautiful garden, ride in his big car and eat all the marvellous food he had often heard described? And what about his family? Will his grandparents be still around when he came back? Who would massage their aching feet with mustard oil? And gentle ammi who spoke so little yet so thoughtful. Won't she miss him?

Thus he sat, he knew not for how long and then slowly got up. He had made up his mind. He went into the room. The quiet rhythmic breathing of his grandparents assured him that they were fast asleep. His ammi however sat on the floor with her knees pulled up and elbows resting on them. Amjad walked up to her. "Ammi, I am not going," he said simply. Was there a hint of relief in her eyes. He could see his mother's shoulders relax in the faint light of the room and knew that he had made the right decision.

CHAPTER SIX

A CUP OF TEA

Aravindan had begun to get hungry again. It was only 4.30 PM. They had had a late lunch today. If he were to tell Radha this, she would chide him. After all, he seemed to be complaining of hunger all the time. Of late he has been like this. Did it have anything to do with the diabetic medicine he was taking? His father had also been likewise but he had been diabetic. As he grew older his appetite seemed to have grown threefold. Now more than ever, he seemed to be bogged down by old memories, especially of his parents and brother Raman kutty.

As a toddler, whenever he cried, it was Ramettan who cheered him. He would carry him and take him around the house, to the cow shed, pluck flowers for him, run around the yard pretending to chase a crow or hen. What carefree days they had been! Ramettan had been the same until the end. Always caring, never would he unburden his sorrows to him but he was there for him whenever he had wanted him. He wiped the tears that had trickled down his eyes. Life was so different then. There were so many people around them, relatives, friends, acquaintances. Now they were so lonely. The only people who visited them were the few remaining friends. Many of them were unwell like them so there were mostly only occasional phone calls.

He walked slowly to the door that opened to the backyard. Radha was among her plants. Today she was well enough to potter around in her beloved garden or whatever was left of it. "Is it time for tea already?" She looked up. "Shall we have it a little later? I am in the middle of replanting the chillies I had planted some days ago. See, all of them are coming up so well!" She pointed proudly.

Sometimes she would be too unwell to water them. If they wilted, she would be heartbroken. So he would go around slowly and water them. Radha had several ailments. But she was a fighter. Anyone in her place would have given up long ago and been bedridden. He was the exact opposite. A mere cold would unnerve him. But now with old age, arthritis had set in and he had difficulty sitting, bending down, and even walking.

He wondered if things would have been better if they had had children. In the early days of their marriage, it had cast a shadow on their otherwise contented life. But slowly they had got over the disappointment. But now of late he often felt that perhaps they should have adopted a child as Radha had often suggested. He was the one who had always opposed the idea. The house would have been livelier. Some days were so dreary with two old souls and their aches and pains. He went back to where he had sat before and ran his eyes through the papers to look for some news that he would have missed.

The aroma of freshly baked cake wafted in from the adjoining house. That made him even more hungry. He wasn't yearning for that. All these modern fads did not appeal to him. Oh, how he longed for the things his mother used to make. He remembered the old dimly lit kitchen, the sunlight trickling in through the tiny windows making a smoky haze, the smoke would make his eyes water. He recalled all the savouries his mother would make, 'Pathiri'* had been his all-time favourite. It had been a long time since he had eaten it.

After Radha's health started failing cooking was minimum. They did buy pathiri once but it was not half as good as what they made at home. That again took him to his childhood days, the fields carpeted below the blue sky, the narrow channels of water they would wade through in which could be found swimming the tiny, translucent fish. How he longed to see all that again! Will he ever see those sights again in this lifetime? Unlikely, he mused.

Maybe he should ask her, he thought. Together they may be able to make a few pathiries. After she had rested a little, he ventured to ask "Shall we make some pathiries?" For a moment she looked vexed. Then her face softened. She knew how much he liked them. "All right but you will have to help," she warned.

Seeing her struggling to open the container which contained the flour, he took it from her. "Why do you close it so hard?" He muttered under his breath. She got hot water ready and together they mixed and kneaded the dough.

Rolling out the balls without breaking it was the trick. Earlier making pathiries had been child's play for her but now it was quite a labour. Finally, they managed to make about twelve pathiries.

It took them quite a while. But they were happy. It had turned out well." We'll save half for dinner," said Aravindan, "will save you the trouble of making dinner," It smelt good. Radha had also prepared the coconut milk to go with it. "Let me keep the water for tea," she said. It was then that the doorbell rang. As she started moving towards the door, Aravindan gestured that he would see, "must be the newspaper boy," he said.

To their surprise, it was their old neighbours, Rukmini and Sreedharan with their little grandson in tow.

"Prateek refused to have his lunch today," said Rukmini as they entered. "Maybe he'll take something from here," Radha asked Prateek whether he would like some pathiries. He looked at his grandmother who nodded. He came and sat down at the table. "Why don't you also join?" asked Radha looking at Sreedharan and Rukmini. Rukmini declined the invitation but Sreedharan gave his grandson company when Aravindan asked again. They ate the pathiries with relish. "Haven't had such pathirees for ages," he said.

They chatted for sometime and as they were leaving Rukmini said, "Hope the pathiries weren't made for dinner."

"No, no," said Radha with a smile glancing at Aravindan who stood quietly near the door.

When Radha closed the door behind them Aravindan went and opened the casserole. A lone pathiri was left.

"I will make tea." said Radha looking at Aravindan's glum face. "Rukmini has brought us some unniappams. It's quite sometime since we had them, looks yum too," she added as she entered the kitchen.

CHAPTER SEVEN

ALL IN A DAY

Padmini was feeling restless. It was almost 11 O' clock. The children had left for school. Her husband had gone to his office. Her maid had not arrived yet. She may not even turn up today. Was it that which was making her anxious? No, there was not much to be done today. She was going to make a simple lunch. Sometimes she had these anxiety bouts as though something ominous was going to happen. Maybe it will pass, she thought. Her aunt was in the hospital but there were people to take care of her.

She entered the kitchen but put back the vegetables she had taken to cut. She just couldn't concentrate. Maybe I'll lie down a bit, she thought. Perhaps she was heading for a fever. But then she decided she needed some fresh air and headed to the balcony. She will also look at the hibiscus she had planted the previous evening.

As she stood looking outside, the phone rang. With her heart in her mouth, she almost ran to take the call.

Beads of sweat stood on her forehead. With clammy, cold hands she took the receiver. "Hello," she managed. It was her husband. All she heard was 'Rahul' and 'hospital'. He had said he was coming to pick her. Had he said 'safe', she wasn't sure. She crumpled in a heap on to the sofa. The rest was a blur....

Vivek ran as fast as his legs would carry him. He had to reach Radhika ma'am. The wind seemed to rush past him. Once he nearly lost a step and lurched forward but steadied himself in time and continued running. The break was over. Children were getting into classrooms. His teacher would be in the classroom now. How will he break the news in front of the other teachers, he wondered. For a moment his mind faltered. Then the vision of the teacher's compassionate face came into his mind. He braced himself. He could not afford to lose courage. He reached the door of the staffroom just as the teacher was entering. He came to a halt in front of her. He was breathing hard. "Ma'am, Rahul is in the water." He pointed to the tank far away.

Radhika ma'am took one look at where he was pointing, threw her books on to the nearest table, called out something to the others and ran followed by some teachers, a peon and Vivek. Somebody went to inform the principal. By the time Vivek and others reached they had pulled out Rahul from among the weeds and pumped out the water. "He is breathing," someone said. He was swiftly bundled into a car and taken to the hospital. Radhika ma'am and some teachers accompanied him. As they started walking back to the school, the principal turned to Vivek and asked him what had happened. Vivek was still in shock. But he explained that they had playfully jostled each other when Rahul fell into the water. He did try to help. He was scared to get in and looked around for a stick but by the time he found one he couldn't find Rahul.

There was some construction taking place in the school. The students had been warned repeatedly not to go anywhere near there. But today unfortunately the workers had not come and the children engrossed in their game of tag, had gone too far.

The principal took Vivek to her room and asked him to be seated. Meanwhile, she called up Rahul's parents and informed them. After that she informed his parents. When his parents arrived, Vivek rushed to their arms sobbing. The principal told them of the accident and then said, "Your son has been very brave. If he had not informed us on time..." He patted Vivek on the back. Meanwhile, they got a call from the hospital that everything was fine but that they would like to keep Rahul under observation and discharge him only the following day. Everyone sighed in relief.

Later at the hospital, a beaming Vivek and Rahul sat chatting with their parents. The Principal and Radhika ma'am too had also dropped by. "Well, well, all's well that ends well. I think I should punish you for going where it's forbidden." She playfully tweaked their ears. "But I hold myself responsible for what happened. I should have posted someone to see that children don't run across there. Or I should have cordoned off the area." She added.

Padmini sat near Rahul and looked at Vivek gratefully. What if he had got scared and not reported the matter? She shuddered at the thought.

CHAPTER EIGHT

MUSINGS

She sat quietly by her mother. Her mother lay inert, quiet and peaceful. The turmoil in her when she had been alive! Her mind raced back to the scene twenty years ago when she had brought her mother home to stay with her.

"Ma, please," she had pleaded. The packing had been over the previous night. Yet they were running late. Her mother had taken ten minutes to walk from the door to the car which was only a few steps away. She had adjusted her sari yet again, opened and closed the handbag, walked to the side of the house as though looking for something till Nalini felt her patience wearing out. Both were silent as the car moved forward leaving behind familiar scenes and memories.

Her mother had been listless since morning. She understandably didn't want to leave the house where she had lived ever since she had got married. She moved from room to room absently patting a sofa back, staring at a picture or peering at something. She was only taking her personal belongings now. They had not decided what to do with the house. Maybe give it for rent later. Her mother picked up a crochet work of Aashu and then replaced it.

Nalini picked it up to put in a cupboard. It would simply gather dust here.

She cajoled her mother to take her medicine, to change and brush her hair. She had hardly touched her breakfast. It was obvious she was heartbroken. But what could Nalini do? It was difficult for her to come to Lucknow so often.

They had no relatives here. Her father had decided to stay on here after retirement and so had bought this house. He had been looking forward to his retirement as he and her mother had made several post retirement plans. One was to come and stay with Nalini in Bhopal for some time. She was expecting and had been advised not to travel. So they were looking forward to spending some time with the baby. Her father had been so fond of children.

Her mind went back to those days. The news had come like a bolt from the blue. She couldn't believe that her father was no more. It had been a heart attack. Now looking at her mother she realized that she had been in a similar state then. She would sit for hours and brood. She had been very attached to him as Ashu had been to their mom. As all form of persuasion did not work, Pramod had requested her mother to come. That had improved matters. Slowly she had come out of her shell. Her mother was so gentle and yet a pillar of strength. She had brushed aside her own sorrow and supported her. That must have taken immense courage, she realized now.

Dad and mom had been inseparable. When her mom had to leave home for something, dad would be totally lost and when dad went away on work it was evident she missed him.

When was it that she had finally started feeling better? They were sitting on a bench, in the garden which she had neglected all these days. Her mom was brushing her hair and she had been absently looking at a shrub of jasmine when a drone of dragon flies came into view. As she watched their zigzag movements, sometimes staying suspended in the air she felt a calmness within. She felt her father's presence. Had he come to see his little girl? Her mom didn't say anything when she shared this thought with her but sat with her everyday watching them as they hovered around and they came everyday till she was hospitalized. Later when Nalini opened her eyes post surgery and felt the warmth of little Preeti nestling against her, was she startled or happy to see the lone dragon fly circling around the room? She looked at her mother whose eyes had filled up.

She had to get her mother back to normalcy, she had vowed. When she was stashing away things, covering mattresses and sofas with Leela's help, she had glanced up at her mother stationed at the window overlooking the garden. This had been her favourite spot. This was where she would stand when they returned from school. Everything would be ready and waiting for them on the table. From here she could see the school bus turning towards their road. Their house was perched a little high up so they could see her too although not very clearly.

The Jambakka* tree was in full bloom. There was a crimson floral carpet beneath it. The previous day to their departure when they were standing underneath the tree, she had asked Leela whether she wanted to take any plants. She only shrugged. Suddenly Leela had shouted excitedly "look! anipille" she looked up to see a pair of squirrels scurrying around on its well spread out branches. The tree was home to these little animals as well as a variety of birds. Nalini joined in her excitement. "Oh, is that what you call it?" She had asked the sprightly Tamil girl. "Tastes yum", she smiled broadly. At first Nalini had been taken aback but then had to smile at Leela's enthusiasm.

It was good to have Leela around. She had been widowed early and lived with her aunt not very far away from home. The only time Nalini had seen her eyes well up was when she spoke about her husband. She would come in the evening, give her mother company for the night, help her with the chores and leave before noon, again to return in the evening. This had been the norm since her father died. Nalini knew Leela would miss her mother but she couldn't accompany her as she had a school going son and an old aunt at home.

Nalini went to stand near her mother at the window. Now standing shoulder to shoulder with her mother she remembered the time when she could barely reach the window sill. It was from her mother that she had discovered the fresh smell of the earth after the first rain. Whenever it rained, they stood there watching the freshly bathed trees, their delicate branches swaying in the wind, light from the house bouncing off its glistening leaves. "Do you know why the earth smells so?" Once Ashu had asked "It's a bacteria Actinobacteria that causes it." Ashu had continued, answering her own query. "What a killjoy you are." Nalini had retorted.

Ashu was the one with the practical head. In so many ways she was like her dad. Calm and strong, a little detached perhaps. Nothing seemed to shake her. When her father died she had not been tearful. She had taken complete charge. She was the one with whom her dad entrusted everything when he left on official tours or meetings. She had taken many responsibilities at her workplace too hence her visits to India had become rare. Her father's demise and Ashu's absence must have added to her mother's loneliness, she felt. Nalini had tried her best to coax her sister to come as frequently as she could since she brought her to Bhopal and she had managed to come a few times.

Her end had been peaceful. All her grandchildren had come for Diwali. She had been very happy. It was a family reunion of sorts. Even Ashu had been able to make it. Mother had sat through the Lekshmi pooja and also sat up with them to watch a movie. She had been her old self. Nalini had never dreamt that she would be able to bring her back to normalcy.

When she had first told her decision to Pramod, he had only asked, "Will you be able to manage?" Nalini had thoroughly thought it out. Each time she visited her mother she felt she was getting worse. She knew it was loneliness that was eating her. Ashu had not been able to come for four years. With her work and kids and the accident she had had, it had been a difficult time for her. So Nalini came as often as she could, usually on weekends. This being the final phase in her career she had been given a transfer closer home.

Nalini's garden had been neglected for sometime. Now that her mother was here, she would get more flowering plants, she made a mental note. It had taken a long time for her mother to even have normal conversations with her. It was as though she had forgotten how to speak. But slowly she had started stepping out of her room. She would sometimes join them in the drawing room. One day she was surprised to see her mother lighting a diya near the tulsi plant. "I used to do this when I was small," her face seemed to glow in the soft light of the diya. But Nalini remembered that her mother had done this even in Lucknow. Had she forgotten? When her mother took up knitting Nalini could see light at the end of the tunnel. It took nearly three years for things to become normal. Old age was also creeping in. But her face shone with energy and happiness which was enough for Nalini.

As neighbours started trickling in, Nalini slowly got up. It was time for her mother to move on. The priests were leaving. Pramod was seeing to them. Nalini turned to look at her mother one last time as she lay seemingly contented, peaceful. "Good bye ma," she whispered soundlessly. A movement near the window caught her eye. She looked up and saw two dragonflies slowly weaving their way out.

CHAPTER NINE

THE BOX

I am one of the few among my cousins who was fortunate to have known my great grandmother. All the children called her 'valliamooma'. She was a source of great joy, wonderment and fascination for us. In spite of her wrinkled skin, her sunken eyes, her hoary hair, we unanimously voted her to be the most beautiful lady in the family. Her face lighted up whenever we came in sight of her and we basked in her warmth and generosity of spirit. There was something more that added to the allure and mystery that surrounded her. And that was a curious little box that sat in her small room.

Ever since I can remember the box had been in her room. It seemed as ancient and lovely as grandma herself. It had beautiful engravings of trees, flowers and strangely, of bears! As we sat around her after dinner listening to her endless tales, my eyes would wander to the box. Come to think of it, it certainly was peculiar that we never asked valliamooma about its contents. Maybe we felt it was empty as it was left unlocked or that it did not contain anything worthwhile. But we felt that it came from somewhere far away.

Sleepily as I listened to her comforting voice my eyes would wander to the box and in my mind's eye I would see myself walking under strange trees, biting into the flesh of even stranger fruits whilst the yellow eyes of a bear would follow me, its arm wrap around me and I would be fast asleep. Valliamooma and the bear thus merged into one. Later I would be dragged to my bed by my parents. The box remained an important part of childhood memories.

Years rolled by. Valliamooma was just a memory. Her things lay untouched as she had left it. Then came the day that the family decided that the house needed a facelift. Walls were broken down. Veranda was widened, roofs were pulled down, balconies were fitted, flooring was changed, things were moved around so much no one knew where what belonged. That was when the old box caught my attention. I looked at it with nostalgia mingled with curiosity. Perhaps it's content would tell me more about valliamooma, I thought. All I knew about her was that she had been brought up in Munnar.

I pulled the box out from under the small rolled up carpet and slowly walked to the window to have a better look. There was a hair brush, some of its teeth had fallen off, a little silver anklet and a fountain pen made of wood. That was all! All of them certainly looked old. I sat gazing them. I knew that what I was looking at was probably my valliamooma's little treasure box knit with her childhood memories most of which she had lost. As I sat there my father happened to pass by. Seeing my dreamy expression and the open contents of the box he came and sat beside me.

"These are valliamooma's," I informed knowledgeably. "I know," he said.

"This is what she was clutching when she was found in Munnar by relatives after the landslide. She had lost her father, mother and younger sister. She had found these among the rubble which had been her home. The bodies were found much later. One of her uncles brought her to his house and it was he who took care of her. She would never part with this box and carried it wherever she went."

I was wonderstruck. I had known so little of her. She who had entertained us with so many stories and blessed us with such abundance of love had such a tragic past!

When I looked at the bear I felt my valliamooma's warm embrace and once more I was the little girl who lay in her lap listening to her soothing voice weaving stories of yore.

CHAPTER TEN

THE RED MUFFLER

She had been his sister's best friend. Ajit couldn't remember when she began invading his thoughts. He felt she reciprocated his feelings. Thus when his parents began to look for a girl for him they didn't have to look far. The matter was discussed, finalized and without much delay the marriage was solemnized.

Everything went smoothly. Meena was just as he had envisaged. She was full of life, laughed easily, got along well with his parents and grandparents, mixed well with relatives and friends. His sister had got married the previous year and lived not very far from their place. She would often come home. They would often visit relatives as both his parents were from the same place and had many siblings. Every little function was like a festival.

His great grandmother had lived to the age of ninety six and had passed away only recently. Since she was staying with them someone or the other would always drop by to see her. The family bonding was strong. Meena said she sometimes envied him as her family did not have any relatives here.

In spite of all this there was something bothering him. He couldn't exactly pinpoint the problem but especially of late he was feeling stifled. Whatever he said in Meena's presence or to her had to be worded carefully. It wasn't that she was very sensitive but that unexpectedly she would sometimes take offence. Earlier he didn't have to think twice before he said anything. There was perfect understanding. If he said that the curry was very nice and if his mother had made it her face fell. But if something Meena made was too spicy or salty, he took care not to comment on it. He found himself being on his guard quite often.

Sometimes it so happened after he came back from work if he found his parents or grandparents in the drawing room he would spend time with them. If he had not asked for her on reaching home, she would get very upset with him and the whole evening would be spoilt. But gradually he was learning the ropes. He knew what upset her and what made her happy and would adjust accordingly. If rice was uncooked he wouldn't complain, if the curry was delicious he would extravagantly praise it. And if the kheer* wasn't even half as good as what his mother made he would down it with great gusto. However much he racked his brains he could not figure out why she was possessive. He wasn't even sure whether it was that.

One evening when he came back from work, he found her very cross. His parents and grandparents had gone to his uncle's place for a pooja. They were supposed to join them later. She had been quite excited about it that morning and had even asked him to choose the saree for her. He wondered what had gone wrong.

She wouldn't have a tiff with anyone. His mother was very diplomatic and handled everything well. Little misunderstandings were smoothened out by his experienced mother. Her sharp eyes had noticed the little changes in him. But she took care not to ruffle her feelings. Sometimes he would be forewarned by her that a particular dish was made by Meena so that he wouldn't blurt out anything.

Although very tired he went across to her. The earlier they sorted things out the better. Peace of mind for him was top priority. At first she refused to say anything. Then he noticed that she was weeping. This seemed like a grim affair. "Was there a call from home?" He asked. "Is anyone sick?" No answer. He went for a wash. When he came back tea was ready. He came and sat next to her. "If you won't tell me I won't know," he said finally. "You know everything. It's just that you don't care," she said. He looked at her baffled. Now, what had he done?

"What was the first present that I had got for you?" she asked finally to what seemed like ages. He tried to remember. "A watch?" He asked." " No, you have completely forgotten." She sniffed once more. He thought again. Then suddenly he remembered and with that, the source of her sorrow also dawned on him. The red muffler!

That morning his mother had been looking for a muffler for his grandfather. The only one he had on was too old. She had meant to buy him a new one but forgotten, thats when he had offered his muffler. He had even put it around his grandpa. "Looking smart, dadu*," he had said. His grandfather smiled the warm, indulgent smile reserved only for his grandchildren. He felt a warm glow within. His grandfather was one of the most even-tempered-people he had seen. His father was quite short tempered but dadu did things in an unhurried manner. He would always have time for them. He was the one who took them to the park when they were children. He was the one to whom he rushed to in tears when as a little boy he got into trouble. Dadu was always there to defend him even when his grandma took sides with his parents. Thus dadu was more like a buddy to him.

"Oh that," he said. He explained the circumstances to her but she continued to be cross so he finally stopped and took the paper and went to sit in the balcony. They had to get ready to go for the pooja but there was still time. This time he was really upset. Why did she have to see things only from her point of view?

Why couldn't she see as he did. After all he always gave in to all her whims and fancies. His family had been part and parcel of his life. Why didn't she understand that? We all have different relationships with one another. One did not take the place of another. If he reciprocated dadu's love that did not affect the love he had for anyone else. His grandparent's love extended not just to the family but encompassed everyone. His friends spoke of them as if they belonged to them. Sometimes he felt Meena was rather selfish and this self-centeredness by her irritated him. But he had to set things right. He couldn't continue like this. He loved his family and they were as important to him as Meena.

Thus he sat deep in thought seemingly reading the paper. She drew a chair and sat next to him. Perhaps she felt that he was hurt. This was the first time that he had shown that he was hurt. But what did she know about them after all? "You know, Meena," he began, "My grandfather had been a totally self-made man. I have told you this before, haven't I? He had struggled quite a bit in his early life. His father had died unexpectedly and although they had some property he had to take care of his younger siblings and life was really difficult. Slowly but steadily he had worked his way up. Then grandma came into his life."

He then went on to relate an incident that had happened quite early in their marriage. "One day grandfather had gone out on work. As he did not come back well past his time and it was getting dark, grandmother had started worrying when suddenly along he comes. She was little taken aback at his sight because it was the dead of winter and his sweater was missing.He explained that he met an old friend who had lost his job. His family was in Calcutta. He was in great financial difficulty, but he had stayed on hoping to get some work but nothing was working out. He had also run out of the money he had saved and did not even have money to buy a ticket back home. My grandpa gave him all the money he had and seeing that he wasn't wearing any warm clothes he gave him the sweater he was wearing. The sweater was a favourite not only because he liked it but was the first one my grandma had knitted for him. So he was a little sheepish about it when he mentioned it. But you know what she said. She said she was very proud of him and she could always knit him another one." Ajit stopped speaking.

It was Meena who broke the silence. "I am also very proud of you. Not because you gave the muffler to your grandpa". She smiled her impish smile, "but for your little story. Come let's get ready now and get going."

Glossary

- dadu - grandfather